ISBN: 978-1-945917-49-3

Printed in the United States of America

Front cover: Detail of Adie Russell's *Shall I Change the Color of the Water* (2018)

Back cover: Detail of Adie Russell's *Shall I Change the Color of the Water* (2018)

Cover design: Kyle Schruder

Black and white photo of Virginia Haggard and Jean McNeil by Charles Leirens. 1947. Courtesy of Jean McNeil

"Making other books jealous since 2004"

Big Table Publishing Company
Boston, MA and San Francisco, CA
www.bigtablepublishing.com

Introduction

In 1946, the artist Marc Chagall, his partner Virginia Haggard, (30 years his junior and pregnant with their son David), and Haggard's five-year-old daughter Jean McNeil moved from New York City to rural High Falls, New York, where they remained for two years. *Beautiful Raft* is the fictionalized story of their experience in the hamlet.

Shortly after my husband and I moved from Brooklyn to High Falls in 2014, I began researching the area and learned that Chagall, Haggard and McNeil had lived in a house five minutes from ours. Their home and the studio where Chagall painted still stand.

I knew who Chagall was, of course, but who was Virginia Haggard? That is the question that launched *Beautiful Raft*.

In historical accounts of their time here, Haggard appears at Chagall's side, a tall, pretty woman often accompanied by her children. Sometimes Haggard is referred to as the maid sometimes as his mistress. Haggard had been Chagall's maid briefly; she was never his mistress. The highly educated daughter of an English diplomat, Haggard spoke several languages and was an aspiring artist herself.

It didn't surprise me that Haggard had been trivialized; partners of famous men often are, and it was the 1940s, yet it angered me. I wanted the women to have a voice in their history with Chagall, so in *Beautiful Raft*, they tell their stories.

After a brief Internet search, I found McNeil alive and well and painting in the UK. She graciously allowed me to use the poem "I Saw Many Things When I Was Small" that she wrote as a child. I discovered the poem in her mother's memoir *My Life With Chagall: Seven Years of Plenty with the Master as Told by the Woman Who Shared Them*. Some of the scenes in the book are loosely based on what I've read and my correspondence with McNeil, who has been generous in sharing details of the family's time in High Falls. *Beautiful Raft,* though, is a work of fiction. Most of the moments are imagined, as are the conversations, inner dialogue, all but one of the letters and several of the characters.

As a former artist, I think visually so as I wrote I imagined the scenery, the clothes, all the bits and pieces. I wondered how other artists would interpret the stories; that's how the work morphed from the written word to the collaborative exhibition *The Virginia Project* (2018-2019). I reached out to fourteen women artists working in a variety of mediums, who each interpreted a different story. Their creations, mounted with my writing, were shown in 2018 at The Wired Gallery in High Falls, just a block from where Chagall, Haggard and McNeil lived. In early 2019, the exhibit traveled to Long Island

University's Brooklyn campus, where it was displayed in the Humanities Gallery.

To see a video, log onto YouTube and search for "The Virginia Project."

Tina Barry,
High Falls, NY, 2019

Virginia and Jean, around 1947

For my mother, Rosalind Ehlin,
who gave us everything.

Thanks to the publications in which some of these pieces first appeared, sometimes in slightly different forms:

Bending Genres: A four-part series about *The Virginia Project*: "Psychosis," "Shadow Pictures," "White Flannel," "Hide Away," "after the measles stop scratching," "Water," "Picnic with Art Dealer's Girlfriend," "High Falls," "Nocturne," "Birth," "Small(er)," and "Raft"

Connotation Press: "Water," "Fortuneteller" and "Picnic with Art Dealer's Girlfriend"

Diaphanous Press: "after the measles stop scratching" and "Virginia Remembers her Maiden Lady Teachers"

Gone Lawn: "Jean's Birthday" and "Exhausted Opera"

MockingHeart Review: included in an interview about *The Virginia Project*: "dad used to hold his hands up"

Mom Egg Review: included in an interview about *The Virginia Project*: "White Flannel," "High Falls," "after the measles stop scratching," "Nocturne," and "Birth"

Olentangy Review: "The Animals Know," "Something Amber," "Psychosis," and "Shadow Pictures"

The Poetry Distillery: "White Flannel" and "Hide Away"

Table of Contents

I Saw Many Things When I Was Small   17

Your Dreams Settle Over My Sleep
    Raft   21
    Psychosis   22
    dad used to hold his hands up   23
    Greeting   24
    Posing   25
    Socks   26
    i tell mum that marc is like a little fawn   27
    I Want   28
    And So   29
    Ballet of the Widowed   30
    Tightrope   31
    i like marcs bathroom   32
    To Implore a Ghost   33
    Nocturne   34
    Oh No   35
    The Rabbit Dies   36
    i think about dad   37
    No Goodbye   38
    Small(er)   39

Even the Stars Pose
    High Falls   43
    Hide Away   44
    Chintz   45
    The Animals Know   46
    This One   47
    i go to marcs studio   48
    Bees   49

30 May 1946   50
Fever   52
Blini   53

My Fate Line is Your Fate Line
Birth   57
I Lunch, I Dine   58
marc buys me a coat   59

but why jean
Our Damp History   63
i am not saying words   64
Poodle Purse   65
9 September 1946   66
after the measles stop scratching   67
Virginia Remembers her Maiden Lady   68
Teachers

I'll Kiss You That Way
15 November 1946   73
A Fowl Finish   74
Thanksgiving   75
Something Amber   76
I See Them   77
Picnic with Art Dealer's Girlfriend   78
Jean's Birthday   79
Play   80
i want to   81
Water   82

The Raft Leaks

    My Small World   85

    My Mistake   86

    Snow Woman   87

    The Raft Leaks   88

    Life   89

    Anxious   90

    Ready   91

    charles is under a big tent   92

    Charles. Charles.   93

Dust Sparkled Birds

    Fortuneteller   97

    White Flannel   98

    Perfect Little Girl   99

    25 June 1948   100

    Exhausted Opera   101

Acknowledgments

Notes

CHARACTERS

Virginia Haggard Artist, 29 years old, married to John McNeil when she met Chagall who was a recent widower

John McNeil Virginia's husband, 35 years old, set designer, who she left for Chagall

Jean McNeil Virginia and John's five-year-old daughter

Marc Chagall Artist, 58 years old, widower

Bella Chagall Marc's late wife. Died suddenly at age 48, shortly before Marc and Virginia met

Ida Chagall Marc's adult daughter

David McNeil Virginia and Marc's infant son. David is Chagall's son but was conceived while Virginia was married to John

Charles Leirens, approximately 60 years old. Belgian musicologist and photographer for *Life Magazine*.

I Saw Many Things When I Was Small

Oh many things I saw
I saw the playroom carpet
I saw the playroom door
I saw my mother get undressed
I saw the cook make cakes
I sometimes saw the other things
But those were my mistakes

~ Jean McNeil

Your Dreams Settle Over My Sleep

Raft

Make my body your raft. A black raft drifting down a
slow, bumping river. A happy raft. Your useful raft.
Climb on, please. Am I big enough? Are you
comfortable? How do I look against the blue water?
Should I change color? Shall I change the color of the
water? I want you to look at me and think, Beautiful
raft.

Psychosis

John's scent settles on the walls, into the torn fabric of the couch; I could mop it off the floors. He sits on a metal chair near the unopened window, knees to his chin and rocks. His hum is tuneless, a distracted bee. I cook what he likes, or once liked, before he became this John: fried cheese sandwiches on thickly sliced bread. A baked potato with a steaming pool of butter. Summer pudding and berries. He stares at the food, frowns. I pull my pants off, stand in front of him, press my bare crotch to his face. He moves his head back, slowly, wincing. *Cat, cadmium, clove*, he says, staring past me. *Potato, cat, cadmium, clove.*

dad used to hold his hands up and make shadow
pictures on the wall   he did a rabbit and a dog   now he
only holds his hands up so we don't see him crying
dad sits on his chair and rocks like it is a rocking chair
but it is not a rocking chair   it goes skritch   skritch
skritch   skritch   dad is a baby now   sometimes I ask
him   will you take me to the park   no sound comes out
but his lips move like mine did when he was teaching
me words   dad would point and say tree   then I would
say tree   then he would point and say squirrel   then I
would say squirrel

Greeting

Ida waits on a bench, tossing crumbs to pigeons, her
hair piled atop her head like a freshly baked croissant. I
hold Jean's hand in mine. Trees in Central Park crown,
an orange umbrella. We walk slowly toward Ida. I want
to appear refined, more than the maid she hopes to
hire. *Please sit*, she says, as we approach, so friendly, as if
we are already intimate. She doesn't seem to notice our
clothing: my wool slacks, Jean's thick tights. Too warm,
even for late October. *I'm Virginia*, I say. *No, you're
Virginichka.* Me an honorary Russian.

Posing

Later, in her studio at Marc's big apartment on
Riverside Drive, Ida poses Jean and me, hand in hand,
on a velvet loveseat. *Two china dolls*, she says. Horns
honk many floors below. As she paints, Ida tells a story
about a party in Paris, where women lounge in satin
dresses. Matisse, Arp, Léger sip champagne. John and I
went to those parties, the young *artistes,* where we lifted
our heads toward the ceiling and blew smoke rings.
Voices raucous with laughter. That John, that Virginia
seem far away. While Ida talks, Marc stands near the
studio door rocking back and forth on slippered feet.
He stares for a moment, nods, then leaves. *My mother
has died,* Ida says.

Socks

Your socks are just as Ida described: black and
huddled, great clumps of coal. Bumping against
strangers with an apologetic smile, I carry the socks
home in a huge hamper. At the apartment, I take one
sock in my hand, it's wool as coarse as black bread.
Limp yet nicely shaped, most of your socks smell only
of wool. A few smell like herring. In each sock, a hole
torn by the big toe. I move to a chair beside the small
lamp, hold a sock to the light, lift the needle and sew.

i tell mum that marc is like a little deer because his eyes
turn up and his curly eyelashes   mum says a little deer
is called a fawn   marc is a fawn with sad happy eyes
marc gives me clay and mum gives me blue beads and
yellow buttons and string and other stuff   i make men
and women and dresses for the women to wear   then
they talk to each other   some kiss   some are in love
then boats go by on the river   i hold up a woman who
would have blond hair if she were real   i think someone
waves

I Want

Virginichka, I want to be talked to, Marc says. He's lonely
for conversation, and Ida's always busy at one gallery or
another. With John, it's: *Don't speak. Don't look at me.
Don't touch me.* Yet Marc is hungry for my words. I sit
beside him at the table. He watches my mouth as if I'll
cast a spell. *Tell me your story*, he says.

And So

Marc emerges from his studio, glances at Jean who has fallen into deep sleep on the sofa. He motions for me to come to him. With both of my hands in his, a long conversation passes silently between us. In it, we acknowledge how Bella's death and John's illness have shaped us; that I am married and a mother. We acknowledge, too, how alive we are to each other; that we want to become lovers. And so we do.

Ballet of the Widowed

Marc stares at a backdrop he's painting for the ballet
Aleko, Tchaikovsky loud and sweeping in the air. *Ah*,
he cries when he sees me, and twirls on one slippered
foot. Then he's dancing, arms bent over his head, toes
pointed and dainty. *Virginichka, please*, he extends his
hand. Still in my coat, I step forward, and, following his
lead, we mince along his studio's dusty floor on tippy-
toes. He releases my fingers, steps back, then runs
toward me. *Attrapez-moi!* he says, arms extended, as if I
were to hoist him in my own. I laugh, raspy and unsure.
Then we both laugh, great whoops and snorts, tears
running. I have forgotten how laughing unknots what's
tamped down inside.

Later, as Jean and I leave to go home, Marc meets us at
the door holding two tiaras he's cut from paper. We
thank him, Jean a bit puzzled; me laughing, again. Marc
sets Jean's tiara on her head and pats her cheek; with
my tiara in place, he lets his palm linger.

Tightrope

I take Jean's hand and tug her down the city blocks.
She doesn't want to go to nursery school. *You'll have a
wonderful day!* I say. We both know I'm lying. I close the
classroom door, pretend I don't hear her calling *Mum,
come back!* and then… I'm a balloon untethered. One
straight shot to the sky. In ten minutes, I'll be in Marc's
apartment. In fifteen I'll be in his bed. When I'm there,
I'm a tightrope walker. A circus in sequins. A tarot card
flipped to the Nine of Cups.

i like marcs bathroom it is quiet   all of it is blue the
toilet too i like to stay there for a long time i do not
have to see anything there   idas bathroom is all yellow
when i am there i am like a big square of yellow butter
melting on a potato   mum comes to the door and says
are you alright jean   i am alright in marc and idas
bathrooms

To Implore a Ghost

Oh, Bella. You stand beside Marc's paintings, and while
my likeness dries on the canvas, you point out its flaws.
Your presence glimmers in the spaces. Even in bed,
when Marc rests his hands in my hair, it's your ebony
halo he touches. Please, Bella. You're with us when
we're talking. You're with us when we're eating. But the
bedroom is no place for our trifecta.

Nocturne

Your dreams settle over my sleep. A great smear of red.
Sun singes my fingers when I touch. Bella. Onyx eyes
and grim pressed lips. Her throat offers a thousand
small wishes. A tornado of birds circle. Boots churn
dust as the Poles threaten a rearranged world. A nun in
white habit makes angels in the snow.

Oh No

A queasy green light cracks through the bedroom's
Venetian blind. One foot and then the other, each
swollen and leaden, finds the floor. I move slowly,
careful not to wake John from his sour smelling sleep.
My brassiere feels tight. So does the waistband on my
skirt. I retch at the smell of an egg boiling on the stove.
First, I think I've caught a flu. But I know. I know.

The Rabbit Dies

John

I go to John. Speak softly. I tell him that his suspicions about Marc and me are true, that because of this new life, the life I share with him is over. John is out of his chair, face purple, hands bunched into fists. I am: liar, whore, Judas. Then he pleads: We, Jean and I, keep him tethered to life.

Marc

I mop and sweep and fold all day, grateful for the busy work. I never peek into Marc's studio or join him for lunch. Before Jean and I leave, I knock on his studio. It's difficult to talk when my heart kicks against my chest. I tell Marc that I must speak to him; I shut the studio door. *What Virginichka?* he says, eyeing me. *Tell me.* He moves close and takes my hands. *Marc, I...*he stares at my face. *Yes?* He says. I am silent; the words won't come. *I am. I am...*He lowers his eyes to my stomach. *Yes?* he says. *Yes,* I say. In the shadows, Bella gasps and turns the room cold.

i think about dad   saying goodbye to dad   i start to
think of dads face   not the way it used to be   the way
it is now   without his eyes seeing me   dad tells mum
he is moving to scotland I hear him yell at mum
come home virginia   mum puts her hands over her
face and cries   i do not want to say goodbye so I walk
slowly   when mum and me get to our old apartment
dad is not there   he is mad that we are late i think he is
mad that I will live with mum and marc   i cry so much

No Goodbye

Jean and I walk up the four flights of stairs. Taped to the door, in John's shaky script, *Forgive me*. His daughter, heart shredded, can come to him but he can't say goodbye. I have spent years feeling sorry for John, now I burn with rage. *What does it say? Tell me!* Jean says. I put the key in the lock and open the door. John's few belongings are gone. In Jean's little room, where two teddy bears once sat on a rocking chair, there is one. Jean notices the missing toy and throws herself onto her bed. She wails. Smacks her face. I hold her hands down. Another torture.

Small(er)

You desire me for my smallness. "Smallness." When I
stand I can look down on your scalp. But that's not the
"smallness" you refer to. You mean "not Bella." Bella
of the opalescent skin. Bella whose body opened to
yours like an eager cleft note to a staff. Whose mind, so
punctuated with color dulled your own. My smallness,
my lesser than, is my gift. For you I make myself small.
Supple. A birch tree easy to bend back.

Even the Stars Pose

High Falls

The real estate agent wears a fedora, smashed almost
flat, a cartoon hat too small for his head. Beneath his
jacket, a shirt stretches so far, the buttons barely hold; I
could rest my hand on the balloon of his belly.

With the windows open, light pours in, a pure yellow
Catskills light Marc will love. We drive from Wallkill to
Bethel, Warwick to Mt Hope. We drive to Kingston,
Cottekill, Olive Bridge and Accord. None of the homes
will suit us.

Your husband's some kind of artist, right? I nod. *Well,* he
says, *I have a house. It's small and kinda beaten down, but it
has another little house next to it. Maybe your husband could do,
well, whatever he does there?*

In High Falls, a small village of wooden homes, cows
graze; cats on front porches turn their bellies to the
sun. He parks the car on a narrow side street. With his
hand on my elbow, we pick our way along, the air
phosphorescent with fir and the clean, mineral smell of
water. *Look up,* he says. Miles above us the falls roar
down as if God had slashed the sky and emptied the
oceans.

Hide Away

I thought I'd die living away from the city's diesel
perfume. Hot dogs' steamy water bath. Pools of dogs'
urine lifted me on my toes. But when I'm here, Jean's
hand in mine, it's as if these new smells—milky cows'
breath. The sweat of nervous chickens. Frogs' exhaled
algae—are an elixir. Our home, snug against the hill, a
stitch of blue before clouds. The road loops and loops
with a long story to tell. Wood smoke curls from barn
wood chimneys. Even the stars pose, waiting for
attention.

Chintz

Flowers outside windows. Flowers in vases. Real
flowers that I can bend over and sniff. My childhood
home had flowers. Chintz-flowered curtains pleated
and puddled on rugs. Roses stabbed, suffocated
beneath thick glass. A grove of wood paneled the walls.
The floors a forest of slaughtered trees. So much color.
And yet, no color. My mother's kitchen scoured of life.
Its cold and tidy heart.

The Animals Know

The squirrel sticks its head from the tree's knot,
shrieking directions, a village gossip with a huge
plumed tail. It moves down the scalloped bark, swaying
on tiny nails, and stops, eye-level with my swollen belly.
A black blur of bird swoops, the velvet of its wing
against my cheek. It nests among a ruckus of robins,
less interested in being fed than being heard. Around
the curve of the road, I near the farmer's fence. His
mare lowers her fan of lashes. In the pond, a fish flips,
exposing its silver stomach.

This One

I tottled when I was pregnant with Jean, a walking
circus tent. Ankles gone. My feet two sandbags. Jean
flailed and rolled, greedy for space, a restless acrobat
inside me. I who knew so little of a mother's
tenderness, imagined porridges and puddings would
appease her. She was John's baby. This baby, this new
life being made, is Marc's. How gently it fills my womb,
content in its saline sea.

i go to marcs studio and sit on the stool that he has for
me   i draw a picture of a cup   it has blue flowers
marc looks and says belle   then i draw a bird with a lot
of feathers   Marc draws too in his book   i say marc
look at my bird   belle he says   then i draw some other
birds   then i draw a rabbit   look I say   marc says
belle   then i draw a cake   look i say but he keeps
drawing   i draw some more but marc does not look
up   i go inside and tell mum marc does not like me
oh jean she says

Bees

Jean has no friends because of Marc and me. The older
man speaking a foreign language. Me pregnant, so
much taller and younger. We smile and wave and
receive a curt nod in response. Our neighbors are a
little warmer to Jean, but not friendly enough to allow
their children to play with her. Now she talks to bees.
She tells me about the insects as if she understands why
they gather outside the window like a convention of
black buzz saws. She stares at the droning clouds and
they stare back, an exchange both private and primal.
She sighs, waves her hand. The insects make an about-
face for the roses.

30 May 1946

Dear Dad,

Mum writes while I say the words.

Mum and me sit on the porch. Mum is hot and waves a big fan in front of her face. Do you know that there is a baby in her stomach? A noisy red truck comes down the street. Marc calls the truck a traveling store because of all the stuff inside it. Sometimes he runs out to buy paint and pencils and talks to the man in Yiddish. I laugh when I hear them. The man has four fingers and a half finger. He sharpens knives, too. "Knives sharpened," he yells. Frieda runs out of her house. "You-hoo! Wait! Wait," she says. Frieda is always running. The man holds her knife against a black spinning wheel until big sparks come out. She sees Mum and me. "How is baby?" she asks.

Marc is mostly nice to me. Are you better, Dad?

Love,
Jean

P.S. Please don't be concerned by Jean's "mostly." It upsets her if Marc looks distracted when she's trying to show him something. Marc and Jean like each other but they're still learning how to get along.

Jean misses you. If you're feeling well enough, please send her a letter.

Virginia

Fever

Tell me everything about your day, you write. Well, Marc, my day is full of waiting: Waiting for your letter. Waiting for the baby to start kicking. Waiting for Jean to wake up. Waiting for Jean to eat her oatmeal. I doubt those small details excite you. This might: I drew.

Late afternoon, Jean, fretful all day, goes to her room. I wait a few minutes thinking she is gathering toys, but when I look in she's asleep. The light falls across her face in a single yellow stripe. She's so precious. So peaceful. I have to capture the sun on her bangs, the bright spot on one cheek.

I run to your studio for charcoal and paper. Absence from the sketchpad makes me clumsy; I hold the charcoal as if my hand is a paw. I draw Jean with the stripe of sun. I draw until her face is fully illuminated. Draw until the sun follows its slow orbit, her face an eclipsed moon. When I'm through—10 sketches, 20 sketches, 30 sketches—pile beside my feet. The joy! I forget how it feels to be awhirl in the moment. To see an eye emerge. A lip's unique imprint. The curve of Jean's delicate hand. I am envious, Marc. You burn with this fever every day.

Blini

Let me show you what I love, you say. You show me
blini. Your eyes lower, tongue swells with memory.
You stand behind me, chin resting on my shoulder.
Take my hands in yours. Eggs brake. Flour sifts
through our fingers.

I will make blini for your return from Paris. Me, your
shicksele. Me of the beans on toast. Yes, blini to
celebrate Chagall the conquering hero. Blini yeasty and
blini floating. Blini in a cape of butter, tipping a caviar
hat.

My Fate Line is Your Fate Line

Birth

Bed of blood and bone. Him her you us. The great usurper who knits himself from me.

I Lunch, I Dine

I see endless people. I can't be alone and work!

and

So many questions from Vollard, Matisse, Léger. There is no peace!

and

I long to come home and work.

and

Don't worry too much about the studio. I need very little; just light, tables and walls, nothing else!

and

I don't feel famous. I'm still the same.

and

I kiss you. You and perhaps David, too.

marc buys me a coat   it has a velvet collar   it is brown
and white weaved together   marc calls it tweed   i lay it
on my bed then i crawl inside and squish up like i am a
baby bird   marc sees a nest in a tree   it is too high to
look inside   marc says eggs blue   that is how he talks
one baby is on the ground   it is not a bird yet   its beak
is open and cracked   it is like david when mum
brought him home   his skin is pink and blue and
white   i want to cover his head with a blanket so i can
not see his open mouth

but why jean

Our Damp History

I'm swollen still. As swollen as an old steamship. I cry for no reason and for all reasons. I cry when Marc pulls the trunk from the closet. Cry when it arrives in the living room, its lid beckoning like a ship no one wants to board. Cry when I smell its damp history and its relief in unburdening it. Soon it will be filled with Jean's clothes and toys. We are sending her to boarding school. *Only for a few weeks*, Marc tells me. *Only for a few weeks*, I tell her. I cry for my weakness. Cry for what the three of us understand: with Jean gone, it's easier for the two of us to love.

i am not saying words because every time i do the girls
at boarding school ask but why, jean and then i think
to myself but why, jean and there is too much to say
too much why and that makes a bad memory   and
then more bad memories like little pictures of happy
things that make me sad now   like looking at dad a
long time ago when me and mum lived with him and
he danced in the kitchen

i make my bed like all the girls in our big room and i
don't stay too long in the bathroom like i did when i
tried to make pigtails   the other girls talk about their
parents and where they have gone and what they are
doing like skiing and all the snow or flying in airplanes
and what they are going to do when they are on
vacation   i do not want to talk about my parents
because there is too much to say and i do not want to
say any of it

Poodle Purse

On Jean's pillow in the big room she shares with five other girls, perches what looks like a toy poodle. Every detail of the dog charms: glass button eyes and a pink stitched smile. Its curly wool fur feels silky in my hands. The nails on its tiny leather paws are painted red. The purse even has that doggy smell.

Jean cradles the bag against her stomach. *I love you*, she whispers, lifting the dog to her lips and kissing it. She barely looks at me. One gift from Marc and she's appeased. I would need a pet shop full of poodles to be forgiven.

9 September 1946

Dear Marc,

Thank you for the purse. When I rip off the gold paper
and the bow, I think that you have sent me a real
poodle. My school friends pet it. I love its face. It
smiles. I like its curly hair and tail, too. I leave the dog
on the pillow when I go to lunch. After, I run back to
the room so it will not be lonely. "I miss you," I say.
Then I kiss it.

Love,
Jean

after the measles stop scratching   my teacher mrs
schwartz takes me to the barnum and baileys circus
she takes me   none of the other girls   this is my first
circus   i am so tired because i can not sleep   mrs
schwartz drives and sings frére jacques and then we
both sing frére jacques   a woman drives next to us and
smiles   i move close to mrs schwartz   I want the
woman to think I am mrs schwartzs daughter

when we get there two clowns are smoking cigarettes
outside   one sees me and squeezes his big red nose
behind a curtain i can see a bearded lady who is smaller
than i am   there are pictures of man twins that share
one body   and dead babies in jars that i do not want to
see   elephants wear flowers around their necks and
march in a circle   one big tiger climbs up a little ladder
a man with a big curly mustache wants him to jump
through a ring of fire   the tiger does not want to jump
so the man cracks the whip

Virginia Remembers her Maiden Lady Teachers

Prudencia

Prudencia? I startle her as she sits at her desk staring at her hand. *Dios!* she says, then begins to cry. Prudencia was married briefly to a wealthy man who divorced her after their year-old son died. My mother sympathizes but fires her with severance and a letter of recommendation. *Grief and teaching don't mix,* she says.

Madeleine and Maude

Madeleine and Maude are a year apart. They have pocked skin and big breasts that feel hard when I lean against them. When I conjugate a French verb correctly, Madeleine says, *Oui.* Then Maude says, *Oui.* When I make a mistake, Madeleine says, *Mon cher. Non, non.* Maude says, *Mon cher! Non, non!* I call them the Parrot Sisters.

Hermosa

Hermosa, small as a child, comes to us from a girls' convent. She wears her hair in plaits. *So fine,* she murmurs, pinching the fabric of my clothes between her fingers. One weekend Hermosa visits a sick aunt. I open the door to her room where I am not allowed. One of my porcelain dolls, eyes snapped open, feet in shiny spats, sits propped against the pillow of her bed.

Justine

Justine wears her dark hair in a tight bun, oily at the
part. She is thirty when she comes to us. Never
married. *Clever girl*, she says, when I recite the times
tables zero to 10. When no one is home to disturb us,
she sits me on her lap and kisses my hands.

I'll Kiss You That Way

15 November 1946

Dear Dad,

I like this school better. Mum lets me walk there by myself. I do not go in the woods; I just look. First, I see trees. If I stand quietly, not even letting out a sound, I see birds and birds' nests, squirrels, and chipmunks. There are bears in the woods, but they hide. Then I'm on Clove Road. Then I walk past the church. Sometimes I imagine people inside sitting on the benches. I imagine me sitting with them wearing a pretty dress and hat. That is how people dress on Sunday when they go to church. They call it their Sunday best. Then I am at the Clove School with the other children. There are nine. Our teacher is Mrs. Brothers. I wonder if she has sisters. That is my joke.

I want you to come to my school for Show and Tell. "This is my dad," I'll say.

Love,
Jean

A Fowl Finish

I don't know what turkeys dream of as they die, but
when my last breath clangs, I'll recall their fleshy
snoods flapping in distress atop their heads. How their
wattles trembled.

Go on, pick one, Frank says. *Don't got all day.*

I hesitate. I had imagined saying, *Oh, 20 pounds or so*,
and Frank doing the choosing. Now I have to
condemn one bird to death. *I can't*, I tell him.

Frank sighs, steps over the pen, grabs an enormous
tom by the neck. The bird flails so violently I wince. He
slams it onto a cement block, bloody with constant
slaughter, ends its life with a single thwack.

I step outside the barn, lean heavily on a tree, while
Frank's wife, splattered jacket over plastic apron, tears
handfuls of the turkey's feathers from its skin.

Back home, I unwrap the bird's still-warm body from
its newspaper shroud, and rock it gently beneath the
sink's cold tap.

Thanksgiving

We sit at the table, artists and their tired wives,
girlfriends in red lipstick, the hungry children. None of
the trauma of the turkey's execution remains on its
amber skin. The women have brought bread stuffing
redolent of onions and ham, sweet yams, but also
gravlax and blini, chopped liver beaded with fat,
herring smelling of long soaks in the sea. We eat and
laugh. Admire infants, new exhibitions, an apartment
with hot running water and cheap rent. There's no need
to mention the spirits hovering. They're here as they're
always here, sniffing babies' fragrant scalps, resting
their cold cheeks on our flushed faces.

Something Amber

The darkened room smells of baby, and cooked lamb.
Over that, the scent of snow. You'd draw my head
differently than I hold it now, cocked like a dumb bird
listening. Jean's breath, not a sound really, just the
opening of air. And David's slight baby rumbling. He's
of you and of me but not. Serious somehow. You
sketched him as connected circles, like the paper chain
you cut from old drawings. We hung it over the table.
Something festive to break up the winter. I like to draw
your hand. The hand with that thumb. Such a thumb!
Wide as the stump of an axed tree. Thoughts of you
make me thirsty. I'll drink something amber. The
glasses' edge etched with your thin cardinal lips. And
kiss you that way. My lips over yours.

I See Them

Silent, unseeing, hands limp in my lap, I imagine the
woods beyond my window, not with its busy animal
village, but alive with those we've lost. I see Bella
hovering in the center; feel you reaching for her, the
perfection of her. She is perfection for me, even as she
diminishes my own. I see the others, too, their
brilliance reduced to frozen rain. I think their thoughts;
remember the heat of their bodies when they encircled
mine. They tease with violets and whisky, then flay my
mouth with wounds.

Picnic with Art Dealer's Girlfriend

The art dealer's new girlfriend, Joan, Inez, Sally?
reclines beneath the cherry tree; it and she are in full
bloom. She's brought a variety of cheeses to share and
watches Marc and me look them over as if we'd banish
her for an unripe Brie. We'd love to ask her how they
met, what she does. But she's listening, eyes wide in
rapture, as the art dealer describes an exhibition in
Amsterdam that *teetered provocatively between the sacred and
profane*. The "Drama Diva" in France, still heartsick
over his defection. And "Only Tuesday," the critic's
lusty wife with one day a week available for a tryst. The
girlfriend lights a cigarette, picks a flake of tobacco off
her tongue. In six months, she'll be the "Silent
Smoker." Until then, she's the one he loves.

Jean's Birthday

The goat hangs like a sacrifice from a tree behind our
house. Boys approach first, slowly, touch its shredded
paper hair of yellow, red and blue. I hand the biggest
boy a stick. He hesitates, eyes wide. *Hit it*, I say,
pointing to the goat. The children understand that the
goat isn't real, but why does it hang and why should
they hit it? *Surprise*, I say, *in the stomach*. The birthday girl
swings. Then two boys grab sticks and whack the goat.
Girls in starched cotton dresses, mouths tense, slam
with as much force as their small bodies allow. Mothers
grab for daughters' shoulders. One father, tall with hair
the color of bleached wheat, grabs a stick and whoosh,
bashes the goat's belly. The children stop, mouths open
in shock, then rush forward as caramels and squares of
black licorice, taffy twisted in waxed paper patchwork
the grass.

Play

Jean won't let me near her when she plays with David. *Go away, Mum!* she says. She carries him in her arms as if he were a little doll. Sets him down on a chair and strokes his hair. If he allows her to, she takes his face in her hands and kisses his cheeks. Sometimes he kisses her back. She sings to him. Reads to him. Rocks him. She loves him, yet I suspect something duplicitous in her actions. Her way of telling me, *Look, Mum. I'm a better mother than you.*

i want to wrap a blanket around david and hold him
like he is my baby

i want to make big bubbles and take david into the bath

I want to draw a picture of david in the bath

i want to dress david in overalls with big buttons

i want david to like my dolls

i want to tell david about the snowmen in the woods

i want to tell david that birds talk

i want to talk like a bird

i want to tell him what the birds say

i want mum to bake us a cake and go away

i want to feed the cake to david

Water

Ida arrives in her city clothes: a hat with a tidy veil, a nipped jacket and tight skirt. I have told her my plans for my afternoon alone: Café. Coffee. Book. *Shoo*, she tells me. *Go! Go!* as the children hug her legs. I don't reveal my real intentions; until I drive to the dirt road and park, I don't know them myself. I walk along a path that twists and twists deeper into the unknown woods. The stones beneath my sandals guide the way. Trees heavy with emerald fringe a rock-trimmed oval of water. I undress with no shame. No fear of being discovered. Cold circles my knees. Then waist. Then neck. My skin contracts, nipples tighten. I'm a long white eel dividing the dark pond. My laugh, high and keening, a child flung into the air.

The Raft Leaks

My Small World

A raccoon rackets about the garbage cans, an owl
works out some conflict in its sleep. I sit at the kitchen
table, my studio; Marc and the children sleep. I've
mixed watercolors. Soft baby hues in porcelain wells:
pale pink touched with brown, washed-down green,
yellow from the sleepy side of the garden. I reach for a
pencil, push the razor's edge along its top. How
satisfying to feel the point against the resistance of
paper, see the first outlines of an animal take shape:
hair-by-hair, ear-by-ear, squinting fox eye, an egg
impatient for its speckled bath.

I tell myself that I create the pictures to amuse Jean,
and when he's older, David, but they're
my small world to share or not to share. It's me they
please.

My Mistake

Pierre Matisse arrives today for his monthly visit. He wears a beret, tweeds; leans against an ivory-carved walking stick he doesn't need. Pierre is a nimble-footed goat. We behave like excitable children hoping for gifts: our voices too hearty, praise too emphatic, the lunch an embarrassment of excess. Pierre heads directly to Marc's studio. He looks over the work, murmurs a few comments: *Mmm, yes*, or *Not yet*. He chooses what he thinks is ready to be sold, often before it's ready to be sold, and after lunch and a short nap on the only comfortable chair, fills his car with paintings.

Today, after Pierre eats and drinks too much wine, he turns to me and asks, *And you, Virginia?* He is being polite. He expects the usual platitude: *Oh, the children keep me occupied*. Instead, I rise and walk to my closet where I store my watercolors of animals. I know I'm foolish to want Pierre to say, *Wonderful! You have such talent!* but I do. Pierre sits at the table with the pile of paintings, studies each one in silence. Marc won't look at me. When Pierre finishes, he says, *Well, something else to keep you busy.*

Snow Woman

I am entombed in this house. Entombed by the
children's desire for entertainment. By the ritual of
dressing, feeding, soothing. By Jean's demands to be
taken outside, and then the donning of long underwear,
snowsuits and jackets. The mittens to be picked up
over and over as they fall. Then the snowballs to throw
and snowballs to pile. Jean wants to make a snowman.
David on my hip, red-nosed, whining. I am red-nosed
and whining. And unseen -- we are unseen -- as Marc
mixes paint in his studio, decides on a brighter blue or
a greener blue. And sketches, and stretches, and
outlines. I want to be in that studio. The children's
sounds unheard. No thoughts of baths or dinner. Just
me.

The Raft Leaks

I have lost the desire to make art. I tell myself that
Marc's needs and caring for the children exhaust me,
and, of course, that's true. And yet, when I was
consumed by the work I could stay awake until
daybreak.

After the children are in bed, I go to Marc's studio to
talk. He turns when he sees me and nods, but he's deep
into a painting, his brush scraping the canvas in a kind
of rage. I long to tell him how much I miss wanting to
make art. That I'm frightened to pull out the paintings
and look at them again. How I fear that the only things
that will ever keep me busy are him and the children.
I'm invisible, I say.

Marc puts down the brushes and comes to me. *I see you*,
V*irginichka*, he says, but his body already leans toward
the canvas. I sit for a moment, then rise to leave. *Finish*,
I tell him, and wave toward the painting of a bride that
looks just like Bella.

Life

Ida is delirious. Charles Leirens from *Life Magazine*
wants to photograph Marc. *Leirens*! she says, breathless
on the phone. Do we know that Leirens photographed
Colette? And André Gide, and Paul Valéry and Bartok?

Leirens arrives in a small, exhausted car. He stands and
smiles toward the house, as if he knows how comical
he appears, this tall man unkinking himself limb by
limb, his cameras, lenses and tripods barely contained
inside. And records, two big boxes of records.

The children rush from the house, already charmed by
this stranger. I have set a table for lunch outside. When
we're seated, Leirens looks at me and then Jean and
David. *Marc is the luckiest of men*, he says. *This woman, these
children.* According to him, David is the most adorable
boy. Jean is a beauty. Jean blushes, looks down. *Right
there*, he points to the apple tree shading us, inhales its
perfume. *And there*, he says gesturing to the field across
the road, *corn*!

During lunch, Leirens listens fully, his eyes locked on
ours. After the meal is served and we drink coffee,
Leirens asks, *Are you an artist too*? I hesitate to answer;
the memory of Pierre's comment lingers. Leirens
touches my hand lightly with his finger. *When you're
ready*, he tells me.

Anxious

Music pours from the open door of Marc's studio:
opera, then Louis Armstrong, who I usually adore;
today the music grates. I'm sick of the children. Sick of
food, even the garnet-skinned tomatoes. Even the
cherry pie.

At dinner, I pour wine. Smile benignly. My breathing
feels unnatural; I'm aware of its shallowness. Twice
Jean asks me something and I don't hear her. I'm
anxious for the children to be asleep. I'm anxious, too,
for Charles to see my paintings.

I leave the dishes, get the children washed and into
their beds. No stories tonight. Marc and Charles are on
the sofa chatting about something; I can't focus. Marc
grows sleepy and with a kiss on my cheek, and a
handshake for Charles, says goodnight. As soon as he's
gone, Charles turns and looks at me, his eyes rich with
warm light. *Ready?* he asks.

Ready

I spread the paintings on top of the table. How juvenile
they are. The rabbits, fox. The little tweeting birds.
Charles holds the edges of each piece carefully, brings it
close to his face. He places several in a row at the top
of the table, then creates a row with the rest. *These*, he
says pointing to the first row, *are exquisite. These*, he says
of the rest, *are simply very, very fine.*

I laugh a bit and begin to cry quietly. *You thought
otherwise?* he asks. I nod and tell him about Pierre
Matisse's remark. Charles waves his hand. *Pierre is a
business man*, he says. *He's only interested in work he can sell.*

We sit on the sofa and talk about how it feels to make
art. I tell him about the late-night painting. How the
moments feel private, and yet there's the communion
with an animal, as if it's a collaborator in the work. He
tells me how he feels when his subject begins to trust
him, how their expression opens, how the picture
seems to frame itself.

The sun cracks through the window when I settle into
bed beside Marc, who has seen all my paintings and
nodded.

charles is under a big black tent   he makes pictures of
marc with a big wood camera   mum hums a song from
the music that Charles brought   mum walks into the
kitchen and says   why am I here   i hear mum and
marc and charles   talking   charles asks mum lots of
questions that make mum laugh   when I take david
into my room to tell him a story mum comes in and
says   why am i here

Charles. Charles.

You held the pink pearl of the conch to your ear and heard me. Oh, Charles, the danger in being heard.

Dust Sparkled Birds

Fortuneteller

Why does a fortuneteller's room smell like salami?
Salami and incense. Strange, I think. And then strange
again, when beaded curtains jangle open and Madame
Shofranka appears. *Ah, you have come*, she says, as if she
knows me. She is a small fox, kohl-ringed eyes darting.
Fingers flit like dust-sparkled birds. I try to ask a
question, but she shakes her head. *Sit.* She places my
hand on her hot palm and stares while it tells my
secrets. When she pulls her hand back, my shoulders
ease; my shame has lessened.

White Flannel

Marc's head blurs above mine. I pull my hips up, wrap
my legs tight. Now he whimpers in his sleep. *Marc*, I
say, shaking him. *Marc*. His eyes are in some bleak
country when he slams his fist in my face. He's awake
now, rushing back to himself. He wants to explain. To
tell me the horrors he's relived. But I hold my hand up.
Something has closed inside me.

Later, while he snores, I dream of embroidering a
picture of his face on white flannel. Careful black
stitches edge the long nose. I color his lips vermillion.
Two thin lines stitched shut.

Perfect Little Girl

Paper Bag

Jean emerges from her bedroom with a paper bag over her head. Her eyes peer from two holes spiked with black lashes. A waxy O of thick red crayon circles the mouth. *I am a baby too*, she says.

Perfect Little Girl

An art dealer and his wife visit Marc's studio to look at new drawings. When they finish, Marc invites them in for tea. Jean changes into her prettiest dress and combs her hair into neat pigtails. She refuses to answer the wife's polite questions, just smiles in a forced way that makes us uncomfortable.

Rabbit

Jean's teacher Mrs. Brothers sews a charming cloth rabbit doll as a going away gift. The rabbit wears a flowered skirt. Jean makes a costume with big paper rabbit ears. I let her cut up an old tablecloth for the skirt. *Oh, look, two dolls!* I say. *No*, she frowns, *two rabbits*.

25 June 1948

Dear Dad,

Mrs. Brothers made a card with a rose on it and gave
me a doll too. The doll is a rabbit wearing a skirt. The
rabbit looks like a stain on my ceiling but with bigger
ears. I will miss the rabbit stain when we move to
France. Is France near Scotland? Will you visit me
there?

Love,
Jean

Exhausted Opera

The neighbors know me here. "Tall gal." A toot of the
horn. A wave. Eyes on the road, moving on. If they got
close, they could probably smell me, as I smell them.
The fraught air of chickens. Cigarettes stale or burning
on the breath. Always, the fat scent of meat. Can my
neighbors smell the man, the children, who feast on
me, ticks on a fat hound? Shouldn't the blue of
delphiniums dim in the dark? Shouldn't the roses'
blousy heads bend beneath the leaves? Crickets hoot a
hypnotic opera. Frogs bleat lovelorn laments.

Barry is the author of *Mall Flower: Poems and Short Fiction* (Big Table Publishing, 2016). Her work has appeared in numerous publications and anthologies, including *The Best Small Fictions 2016*, *Drunken Boat*, *Blue Fifth Review*, *The American Poetry Journal*, and *Nasty Women Poets: An Anthology of Subversive Verse*. Barry has been nominated for two Pushcart Prizes and several Best of the Net awards. She is a teaching artist at The Poetry Barn and Gemini Ink. Visit her at TinaBarryWriter.com.

Notes

"I Saw Many Things When I Was Small" is reprinted with the permission of Jean McNeil. The poem first appeared in Virginia Haggard's *My Life With Chagall: Seven Years of Plenty With the Master as Told by the Woman Who Shared Them* (Donald I. Fine, Inc. 1986).

Lines from "I Lunch, I Dine" were taken from a letter. from Chagall to Haggard. *My Life With Chagall: Seven Years of Plenty With the Master as Told by the Woman Who Shared Them* (65).

I referred to Haggard's book as well as *Chagall* by Sidney Alexander (Putnam, 1978) for historical background.

I am grateful to Jean McNeil who graciously answered questions and provided some details.

Acknowledgments

I want to thank my writing group who cheered this project on: Anique Sarah Taylor, Lissa Kiernan, Sharon Israel Cucinotta, Mary Savage, Jerrice Baptiste and Alison Koffler-Wise. My beautiful daughter, Anya Brosnan, and my mother, Rosalind Ehlin. Special thanks to Sevan Melikyan of the Wired Gallery, who said yes to the show and became a friend. Nancy Grove the curator at the Humanities Gallery at Long Island University, for exhibiting the show, and for all her generosity over the years. Thanks to the committee at the Woodstock Byrdcliffe Guild for the residency in summer 2018, during which several of these pieces were written. Special thanks to Virginia Haggard, and especially Jean McNeil, who inspired this book and *The Virginia Project*, and whose lives I interpreted so freely. And always to my husband, Bob Barry, who has a unique talent for being a perfect partner.

CPSIA information can be obtained
at www.ICGtesting.com
Printed in the USA
LVHW041255151019
634129LV00028B/6335/P